It's Father's Day, Charlie Brown!

Based on the comic strip and
characters created by Charles M. Schulz
Adapted by Judy Katchske
Art adapted by Tom Brannon

LITTLE SIMON
New York   London   Toronto   Sydney

 LITTLE SIMON
An imprint of Simon & Schuster Children's Publishing Division
1230 Avenue of the Americas, New York, New York 10020
© 2004 by United Feature Syndicate, Inc. All rights reserved.
PEANUTS is a registered trademark of United Feature Syndicate, Inc.
All rights reserved, including the right of reproduction in whole or in part in any form.
LITTLE SIMON and colophon are registered trademarks of Simon & Schuster.
Manufactured in the United States of America
First Edition 10 9 8 7 6 5 4 3 2 1
ISBN 0-689-86819-7
Based on the comic strips by Charles M. Schulz

It was Father's Day! Charlie Brown and the Peanuts gang had only one thing on their minds . . .

Their dads!

"What did you get Dad for Father's Day?" Charlie Brown asked his little sister Sally.

"For what?" Sally asked.

"For Father's Day!" Charlie Brown repeated.
Sally's eyes popped wide open. "I thought we just had Mother's Day!" she gasped
"That was last month," Charlie Brown said.
"What about Valentine's Day?" Sally asked. "What happened to Valentine's Day?"
"That was in February," Charlie Brown said.

Sally couldn't believe it. Where had the time gone? What happened to Christmas? And Easter? And Groundhog Day?

"What happened to my birthday?" Sally asked.

"Your birthday doesn't come for two months yet," Charlie Brown explained. "First comes the Fourth of July."

"*Then* my birthday?" Sally asked.

Charlie thought Sally was missing the point, so he decided to give it another shot. . . .

"So," he asked Sally a second time, "what did you get Dad for Father's Day?"

"For what?" Sally asked again.
Good grief!
Charlie Brown decided to figure out the perfect Father's Day present all by himself.

Peppermint Patty had Father's Day all figured out. She decided to celebrate the big day by calling her dad on the telephone.

"Hello, Dad?" Peppermint Patty said into the receiver. "I just called to wish you a happy Father's Day!"

But it wasn't Peppermint Patty's dad on the other end of the line.
It was Charlie Brown!
"Who are you calling?" Charlie Brown asked.
"What?" Peppermint Patty cried.
"I said who are you calling," he asked again. "Who is this?"

Peppermint Patty would recognize that voice anywhere. It was Charlie Brown! "Chuck!" Peppermint Patty shouted. "What are *you* doing there?"

"I'm not there—I'm here," Charlie Brown explained. "I think you dialed the wrong number!"

The wrong number? Peppermint Patty didn't want the wrong number. It was Father's Day and all she wanted was her dad!

"Chuck!" she shouted. "You always spoil everything!"

But nothing would spoil Lucy's Father's Day!
"What are you doing?" Charlie Brown asked. Lucy held
up the blue and white construction paper she was cutting.
"I'm making sort of a Father's Day card," she answered.

Charlie Brown was impressed!

"That's great!" he told Lucy. "I'm proud of you. Father's Day doesn't get the recognition it deserves!"

Lucy kept on cutting and pasting.

"I find that it is all too frequently ignored!" Charlie Brown went on.

"Thank you!" Lucy told Charlie Brown. Then she
began to write . . .
   "Dear Mom—have a Happy Father's Day!"
Charlie Brown rolled his eyes.

Snoopy had written a letter too! His was already signed, sealed, and ready to be delivered to his dad. Snoopy sat on top of his doghouse. But he felt on top of the world!

"For your dad, huh?" Charlie Brown asked.

That's right, Snoopy thought. *For Father's Day!*
Snoopy jumped off his doghouse. Then he carried his Father's Day card to the mailbox. *I just found out that he's retired now and living in Florida,* Snoopy thought. *I know he'll appreciate getting this card.*

Snoopy was right.
And they all *signed it!* Snoopy's dad thought happily.

Charlie Brown still hadn't figured out what to give *his* dad for Father's Day. So when his dad came to his baseball game, he decided to do something he had never done before.

He decided to *win*!

"I'm dedicating this game to you, Dad!" Charlie Brown shouted as he pitched the ball.

"Happy Father's Day!"

But when it came back . . .

Charlie Brown stared up at the sky. He felt like a loser in front of his dad, and he *looked* like one too!

"Maybe I should just get him a necktie," said Charlie Brown. But finally he realized that it really didn't matter. . . .

"See this?" Charlie Brown said to Violet later that day. "This is my dad's barber shop."

Violet stared at the little shop. It had a barbershop pole outside with red and white stripes.

"I can go there anytime," Charlie Brown said. "And no matter how busy he is, my dad will always stop and give me a big smile."

Charlie Brown had learned an important lesson.
It's not the present. It's the *person*! Happiness is
Charlie Brown's dad!
　　And Peppermint Patty's dad!
　　And Lucy's dad!
　　And even Snoopy's dad!
　　No matter *what* day it is!